The Dunkard

The Dunkard

by~ George Selden

pictures by~

Peter Lippman

x

Harper + Row, Publishers

New York, Evanston, and London

Grown-ups Day at Our School

1. George
2. The Dunkard
3. Miss Brill
4. Doctor
5. Dentist
6. Veterinarian
7. Secretary
8. Policeman
9. Fireman
10. Poet
11. Acrobat
12. Other
      Grownups
13. Children

Chapter One

I Hunt for My Grown-Up

I love to dunk!

And because I do, I won first prize in Grown-Up Day at school last week.

Every year our school has Grown-Up Day. The boys and girls each bring in a certain kind of grown-up who has a certain kind of job. It doesn't have to be your father, or even an uncle—just some grown-up who has a job that you think is very interesting.

Miss Brill, our teacher, gets very nervous on Grown-Up Day. She wants everybody to like our school, and parents are invited to come and watch. Parents and aunts and people like that. All afternoon before Grown-Up Day Miss Brill keeps interrupting lessons. Her head bobs up from the book she's reading, and she says, "Oh, I hope everything goes off all right! You *will* behave, won't you, boys and girls?"

And all of us murmur, "Yes, Miss Brill."

Then her head bobs down again.

One boy or girl and his grown-up get voted first prize. And after the ceremonies are over, everybody goes down to the school cafeteria and we have a special lunch.

But it isn't very exciting after the first few times. You see so many doctors and lawyers and policemen and people you've seen before. They're all very nice, and "highly respectable," as Miss Brill says. But I wanted to meet someone *new* one time!

The year before this one I tried to bring in a hobo, but Miss Orm stopped him at the door. Miss Orm was my teacher last year. So I had to run out and come back with just a mailman. I liked that hobo a lot though. He gave me a red bandana that he'd brought all the way from Arkansas.

On the day before this year's Grown-Up Day I made up my mind that I wouldn't even come to school unless I could find the most interesting grown-up that anyone had ever seen.

As all of us were filing out we heard Miss Brill say, "Oh, dear! I do hope everything goes well tomorrow! Make *good* choices, won't you, boys and girls?"
We all murmured, "Yes, Miss Brill."

The whole town was full of boys and girls who were hunting for their grown-ups.

First I walked past the police station.

Then I walked past the firehouse. (Firemen love to be asked to come to school on Grown-Up Day.)

And I walked past a big office building that was full of all different kinds of businessmen and salesmen and secretaries.

I really walked a long way. Past a church where the minister looked awfully eager.

And out past the houses on the outskirts of town. One housewife even tried to bribe me with cookies. (We see dozens of housewives on Grown-Up Day!) But I just no-thanked her politely and kept on walking.

I got way out into the countryside.

And I still couldn't find the right grown-up.

At last I came to a patch of poplar woods where I had never been before. A funny little round house was standing among the trees. And inside the house somebody was singing.

I went up close, to hear the words.

Oh, dunking is a joyous thing...

I peeped through the window, and inside that house was one of the happiest-looking grown-ups I had ever seen! He wasn't exactly fat, but he certainly wasn't thin. And he wasn't exactly old, but you couldn't say he was young. Sort of chubby and middle-aged he was, with a very jolly face. And he was sitting at a table, dunking a doughnut in a cup of coffee.

He saw me peeking and said, "Good afternoon! Do you like to dunk?"

"I love to dunk!" I said.

He gave me a wink and a grin, and said, "Come in and dunk a while."

So I did.

Chapter Two
I Find Just the Right One

The whole house was like a big kitchen and living room combined. There were cups and glasses—for dunking—all around. And there were lots of cupboards and refrigerators, all full of food to dunk.

"Since I have company," my new friend said, "I'm going to fix us a meal."

Well, first we had split-pea soup. Awfully good! But when I started to eat mine with a spoon, he said, "Oh, no! Not like that. What you do is, you take a piece of bread and you *dunk* your soup up!"

He showed me how. It took quite a while before I
learned to do it without spilling, but my friend did it
perfectly.

19

Then we had spaghetti, which I like very much! But instead of the usual way—with the sauce poured on top of it—what we did was, we wound up the strands of spaghetti on the ends of our forks and then *dunked* them in the sauce! It tasted even better like that.

For dessert he brought out a big bowl of Jell-O. "Well," I thought to myself, "at least you can't dunk Jell-O." But I was wrong. Because he brought out another bowl, full of beautiful sweet whipped cream, and we both dunked spoonfuls of raspberry Jell-O in it. Oh, boy!

I never knew there were so many things you could dunk. He told me that when he had lamb chops, he dunked them in mint jelly. "And when I have a hot dog, I dunk it in mustard. And lobster in melted butter—"

"I do that too," I said.

"Yes, but do you dunk salad?" he asked.

"I'm not so great on salad," I admitted.

"Try dunking the lettuce in the salad dressing. You'd be surprised how good it can taste."

And he showed me all the ways to dunk. With right
or left hand, and how you tap the last drop away so
as not to spill, and everything like that.

It was a very happy time for us both.

Finally I said, "By the way, what kind of a grown-
up are you?"

"I am a dunkard," he said.

"Yes, but what is your job?" I asked.

"I dunk."

"No, but"—I tried to think of that word Miss Brill is always using—"what is your *occupation*?"

"Dunking!" he said.

"Well, but dunking doesn't make you any money," I said.

"It may not make me money, but it makes me happy!" he answered. "I'll tell you how it happened. Years ago I used to be an office worker. I sat behind a desk and did...well, I forget what I did. It was just some kind of office work. The only thing I really enjoyed about it was the coffee break. Then I could stop my office work and have a cup of coffee and something good to eat. And whatever I had—a doughnut, say—I always dunked in my coffee. Well, one morning I was musing over a Danish pastry, and suddenly I realized that I wasn't an office worker at all. I was really—"

"A dunkard!" I exclaimed.

"A dunkard." He nodded and sighed blissfully. "I stood up from my desk and my office work, I walked out of the building, and I never went back. I had saved up enough money to build my little house out here, and here I've been living ever since."

"Dunking and eating," I said.

"Yes," he answered. "But you have to understand one thing. I don't dunk so that I can eat. I eat so that I can dunk!" He put one hand over his heart. "It's my Calling and my Way of Life."

Right at that moment I got my big idea. "Hey, Mr. Dunkard," I said. "Will you do me a favor tomorrow?"

He gave me a wink and a grin, and said, "Maybe."

Next morning I got up very early. I had to walk
all that distance to go get the dunkard.

I bundled him up so you couldn't see who was
under the clothes, because I wanted him to be a surprise in the classroom.

Then I took him to school.

Instead of bringing him to the usual room where all the grown-ups wait, I hid him in the cellar, to make sure that he would be a surprise.

And Grown-Up Day began.

Chapter Three

Grown-Up Day

What happens is, a boy or girl goes to get his grown-up and brings him into class and says, "My friend is a doctor!" Or a lawyer or whatever the grown-up happens to be.

Mary Jane Anders was first. She brought in her grown-up and said, "My friend is a secretary!" And the secretary typed on her typewriter awhile. (The grown-up is supposed to show what he does or else give a little speech about it. Then afterwards we clap.)

Bobby Cadmus brought in a fireman who started a fire in a metal wastebasket. That made Miss Brill pretty nervous. But the fireman put it out with his extinguisher. All clapped.

Then Francis Gunderson came in with his grown-up and said, "Um—my friend is a dentist. I guess." Everybody tried not to groan, but it was a hard and gloomy time for us all. The dentist didn't drill anybody though—just showed us how to use dental floss. A few clapped.

So far the competition had not been too bad. But when Louise Mikler brought in a veterinarian, I began to get jittery. Because this veterinarian had a big friendly woolly dog with him. The dog went up and took a sniff at Miss Brill, which made her even more nervous than the fire had. But the boys and girls loved him. The veterinarian made him swallow a pill for worms. All clapped.

But the next grown-up *really* worried me. David Potter stood at the door of the classroom and announced—sort of boasted, in fact—"*My* friend is an acrobat!" And in bounded this acrobat, all dressed up like the circus. He did handstands and cartwheels all around the room, and ended up with a double somersault in the air! All clapped and shouted. Except me. I worried.

I was jumping out of my skin with impatience, waiting for my turn to come. But I had to sit through two doctors, a hairdresser who gave Betty Quish a permanent wave, and a very skinny poet who wrote a little poem. Thompson comes near the end of the alphabet. (That's my name, by the way, George Thompson.) And I was last this year.

Finally Miss Brill said, "And now, George Thompson."

I ran out of the room, down to the cellar, unwrapped the dunkard, and led him back to class. And in a big loud voice I said, "My friend is a DUNKARD!"

"A *what*?" said Miss Brill, getting ready to be very nervous again.

"A DUNKARD!" I said. "Now wait! Just wait!"

I ran back down to the cellar again, where I had hidden some bread and milk. (It was all I could snitch from the kitchen that morning.) And I brought it up to class. "Now show everybody!" I said to the dunkard.

He sat at Miss Brill's desk and began to dunk— very beautifully too. And as he dunked, he sang a dunking song:

> *Oh, dunking is a joyous thing,*
> *A genuine delight.*
> *It makes you want to laugh and sing.*
> *I dunk both day and night!*

Well, as I had hoped, the dunkard was a big surprise to everybody. And a shock to some, I could say. The grown-ups all gawked at one another, and Miss Brill was just bubbling with confusion. But the dunkard only went on dunking and singing his dunking song:

To dunk not only cancels out
All loneliness and pain,
It helps the looks, cures colds and gout,
And also aids the brain.

Now right at this moment I thought I saw a smile come on Miss Brill's face. But she quickly tried to hide it. (I like people who try to hide smiles, especially when they can't.) The dunkard must have seen it too, because he aimed the next verse of his song right at Miss Brill.

I know some say, "Ridiculous!"
They scoff and they deride.
But honestly that's just because
They've never even tried!

"But—but—but—" Miss Brill began to say something. Only she forgot what she was going to say.

"But what, my dear?" said the dunkard politely.

"Well—I mean—we wanted to meet grown-ups with *serious* occupations," said Miss Brill.

You could tell she had hurt the dunkard's feelings. He looked at her painfully and said, "How *can* you say such a thing, Miss Brill?" Then he rose to his feet and sang, *very* seriously:

> *A solemn study is this dunking,*
> *A grave and glorious art.*
> *It's not just splashing and kerplunking,*
> *It must come from the heart!*

By this time Miss Brill was having real trouble trying to hide that smile. In fact, from what I could see of it, it looked like a downright laugh. "I understand," she said quietly. "But isn't dunking rather—if you'll excuse me—rude?"

My heart tightened up like a rubber ball when I heard her say that. Suddenly the thought of parents, and especially my mother, flashed angrily past. Because I realized that nobody could ever win first prize for doing something rude.

But I hadn't taken into account how clever the dunkard was. He merely looked down at Miss Brill and said, "Tut-tut, my dear. It isn't rude the way *I* do it." Then he sang another dunking song:

> *One dunks in coffee, milk, or tea,*
> *One dunks in* any *company*
> *As long as one dunks gracefully!*

When he finished singing, he leaned over very close to Miss Brill's head and almost whispered, "Now tell me, dear Miss Brill, and be honest. Wouldn't you like to dunk a bit yourself?"

A hush fell over the room. And the dunkard began singing again. (He must have made this song up right on the spot.)

> *Miss Brill, do try a little dunk.*
> *Your soul in bliss will soon be sunk.*
> *If not, then tell me it's all bunk.*

He paused, which made a very dramatic effect. And then, with outstretched arms and his voice full of feeling, he sang the last two lines:

> *Oh, dare, Miss Brill! Dare take that dunk!*
> *Then pass me. Or then let me flunk.*

Chapter Four

First Prize

There was a shocked silence. And all of a sudden Miss Brill's laugh escaped completely. She began to blush and giggle!

Well, none of us had ever seen our teacher either blush *or* giggle, or even laugh very much. And there she was, sitting in front of the whole class and grown-ups and guests too, just tittering away.

When she got control again, she sort of murmured to the dunkard, "As a matter of fact I believe I *would* like to try a dunk, if I may."

Without a word the dunkard reached the bread and milk over to her. And she gave the daintiest little dunk you can imagine! All clapped. In fact all stood up and cheered!

The dunkard looked out over the audience and said, "And all the rest of you here—doctors, lawyers, acrobats, dentists, veterinarians, and various whatnots—don't all of you like to dunk too? And wouldn't you like to be dunking right now? Be honest, friends! Deep down now, wouldn't you?"

For a moment no one said anything. Then a big
shout of "YES!" went up.

Was I ever happy!

The dunkard and I got voted first prize. The fireman and a policeman hoisted him up on their shoulders and carried him around the room. And Mike Noldy and Jim Kimble hoisted me up on their shoulders and carried me around the room.

Then we all went down to the cafeteria for lunch. Everyone was thinking of only one thing. And it worked out too, because we had hamburgers—which you can dunk in a little puddle of ketchup on your plate.

I was sitting on one side of the dunkard and Miss Brill was on the other. For a while they both talked to me, but then they began to chat with each other. I didn't mind though. I just sat there and was glad all by myself.

Everyone agreed it was the best Grown-Up Day that we have ever had.